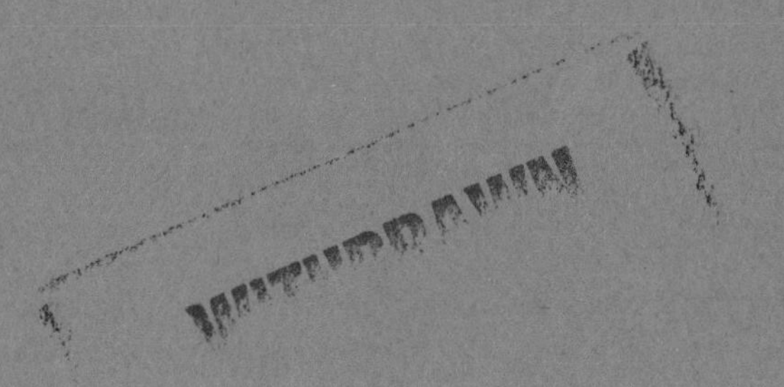

CARNIVAL AND KOPECK

and more about Hannah

Illustrated by Karen Ann Weinhaus

CARNIVAL AND KOPECK

and more about Hannah

by Mindy Warshaw Skolsky

Harper & Row, Publishers

New York, Hagerstown, San Francisco, London

 Printed in the United States of America. For information address Harper & Row, Publishers, Inc., 10 East 53rd Street, New York, N.Y. 10022. Published simultaneously in Canada by Fitzhenry & Whiteside Limited, Toronto.

FIRST EDITION

Library of Congress Cataloging in Publication Data
Skolsky, Mindy Warshaw.
Carnival and kopeck and more about Hannah.

SUMMARY: When Hannah and her grandmother have their first quarrel, Hannah learns that living near someone you love sometimes makes problems.
[1. Grandmothers—Fiction] I. Weinhaus, Karen Ann.
II. Title.
PZ7.S62836Car 1979 [Fic] 77-25643
ISBN 0-06-025686-9
ISBN 0-06-025692-3 lib. bdg.

To my uncle, Morris J. Markowitz,
and to the memory of Uncle Louis and Uncle Abe—
the original Hannah's three sons

MORNING: THE SPELLING LESSON

It was the first day of summer vacation. Hannah ate a big stack of pancakes with maple syrup for breakfast. Then she put on her tap shoes and kissed her mother good-bye.

"Why are you wearing your tap shoes?" asked her mother. "There are no dancing lessons in the summer."

"But I still love to tap-dance!" said Hannah. She jumped up in the air and clicked her heels together. Then she tap-danced out the door and down the street to her grandmother's house.

Along the way, she came to a big sign tacked to

a leafy tree. Hannah stopped dancing and went over to read it. She read: "CARNIVAL IN THE PARK TONIGHT."

"A *carnival*!" yelled Hannah. She ran the rest of the way to her grandmother's house. When she got there, she opened the screen door and let herself into the kitchen.

"Grandma!" said Hannah. "There's a *carnival* in the park tonight! Will you take me? Ugh, I smell fish!"

Hannah's grandmother put down the knife she was chopping fish with.

"I think it will be too late for you to stay up," she said.

"But I have no school tomorrow," said Hannah. "It's summer vacation."

"Then it's all right with me if it's all right with your mother," said Hannah's grandmother.

"Oh, Grandma," said Hannah. "I'm so glad you and Grandpa moved out here to Nyack! I hope you stay forever!"

"Nothing stays forever," said Hannah's grandmother, "but I'm glad we're here for now. Don't let the screen door slam, Hannah!"

But Hannah didn't hear her. She was too busy running back up the street.

"Grandma says she'll take me to the carnival tonight if you say yes," she told her mother.

"Yes," said Hannah's mother, "but calm down. You're all out of breath. You know it isn't good for you to get overexcited."

"I know, I know!" said Hannah. "Hooray—I can go!"

She started to run back down the street to tell her grandmother. On the way, she saw Otto Zimmer reading the sign on the tree.

"Hey, Otto—I'm going to the carnival!" called Hannah.

"Oh, yeah!" said Otto. "Who's taking you?"

"My grandmother," said Hannah.

"Oh, yeah!" said Otto. "I'll bet. After the strawberry festival? I'll bet she is!"

"Don't you say 'strawberry festival' to me, Otto!" said Hannah.

"Strawberry festival, strawberry festival!" said Otto. "Hannah got sick at the strawberry festival! Besides, your grandmother never comes out in the street. My mother says she's stuck-up!"

"Don't you dare say that!" said Hannah. "I don't know why I talk to you, Otto." She started to run again.

"I am *so* going to the carnival with my grand-

CARNIVAL
IN THE
PARK
TONIGHT

mother!" she called back over her shoulder.

Otto made a loud noise. "Raspberries!" he yelled after her.

Hannah ran back to her grandmother's kitchen. Her grandmother was still chopping fish.

"Grandma!" said Hannah. "She said yes! Ooh—I can't stand that Otto Zimmer!"

"Don't even associate with such people," said Hannah's grandmother. "I never see this boy do anything useful at all. He just makes insults and blows raspberries. So we'll go to the carnival tonight. But you have to promise not to nag me for junk like hot dogs. Remember the strawberry festival."

"Oh, Grandma—don't you say it too," said Hannah. "Otto just reminded me. I feel embarrassed when I think about it. The strawberry festival was the first place we went together when you moved out here last spring. I was so excited I forgot to eat just strawberries like my mother told me. Hot dogs look so good and taste so good, I always forget I'm not supposed to eat them—but I won't forget tonight."

"And besides the hot dogs, you kept calling over all the neighbors to meet me," said Hannah's grandmother. "Your neighbors give me a headache with so much loud talking."

"I *wish* you'd come out and talk in the street sometimes like the other neighbors, though," said Hannah.

"No talking in the street for me," said Hannah's grandmother. "I don't like it. So if fresh Otto just reminded you about the strawberry festival, I won't say any more. I don't want you to feel embarrassed. Only if we go to the carnival, you absolutely positively must remember three things: No getting excited. No nagging for hot dogs. And no calling neighbors over."

"I promise, I promise!" said Hannah. "Grandma, if you take me to the carnival at night with the lights and the music and the merry-go-round, I'll promise anything!"

"How about promise to taste my gefilte fish when I finish it?" Hannah's grandmother joked.

"Grandma—please!" said Hannah. "I promise anything else but that. You know I can't stand fish." Hannah held her nose.

Then she said, "Tell me a story—I can't wait!"

Hannah's grandmother put her knife down again. "Since I moved to the country, all I'm doing is telling stories and playing school," she said.

"That's why I'm so glad you and Grandpa moved out here!" said Hannah. "Stories and school are so much fun!"

"Fun is fine," said Hannah's grandmother. "But who is going to do my work?"

"I'll help you later," said Hannah. "With anything but fish. Fish makes me gag. I'll help you bake."

Hannah's grandmother looked at Hannah and she looked at the fish. She thought a minute.

"People before fish," she said.

She put the fish in a dish and covered it. She put it in her icebox. She made hot foamy soapsuds and washed the knife, the top of the table, and her hands.

Then she sat down at the kitchen table and said, "Okay, teacher, *play school*!"

"How about a story first today?" asked Hannah.

"School is first," said her grandmother. "The story will be second."

"But we always do it that way," said Hannah. "In school, Miss Pepper always does things in the same order too. Why can't we do it the other way around sometimes?"

"Because education always comes first," said her grandmother.

"Sometimes it would be fun to change a little," said Hannah. "But all right. I love being the teacher too. Call me Miss Pepper."

Hannah stood on a little step stool. She took a big

red box out of the kitchen cabinet. On the box was a white label with blue around the edges. On the label it said, in Hannah's best lettering, "SCHOOL."

Hannah opened the box and took out a sheet of paper with lines. Then she found a pencil with a sharp point at one end and an eraser on the other end. She gave the paper and pencil to her grandmother.

Hannah clapped her hands together.

"Attention, class!" she said. "Miss Pepper is going to give you a test. First the heading. On the top line, write your name. Write it on the left side."

Hannah's grandmother wrote "Trudy."

"Now on the same line, write the date. Write it on the right side."

Hannah's grandmother wrote "June 27, 1932."

"Keep it neat, Trudy," said Hannah. "Neat penmanship is very important."

Hannah's grandmother wrote slowly and carefully. She leaned so far forward, Hannah could see the bun at the back of her neck and the little speckled comb that held it in place.

"Remember good posture," said Hannah. "Sit up tall. No writing with your nose. Now the words. Number to ten on the left side, and don't forget the margin."

Hannah looked at a book. She picked it up. "This is the first word on the spelling test," she said. "Book."

While her grandmother was writing, Hannah got a hat out of the hall closet.

"This is the second word," she said, holding it up. "Hat."

Hannah's grandmother wrote very slowly.

"Keep up with the class, Trudy," said Hannah. "Miss Pepper doesn't like people to fall behind."

Hannah held up her hand. "This is the third word," she said, looking at her grandmother. "Hand."

"Four," said Hannah, pointing to herself. "Me."

"Five." She pointed to her grandmother. "You."

While Hannah's grandmother was writing, Hannah took a big piece of drawing paper from the school box. She drew some pictures. She cut them out. She held them up, one at a time.

"Six," she said, showing one of them. "Girl."

"Seven." She showed another. "Boy."

"Eight," said Hannah, holding up the next one. "Cat."

"Meow," said Hannah's grandmother.

Hannah clapped her hands together. "No talking during a test," she said. "You know the rules in this classroom, Trudy. Miss Pepper is *strict*!"

Her grandmother wrote "cat."

"Nine," said Hannah. She held up the last picture. "Dog!"

Hannah's grandmother barked.

"Trudy!" said Hannah. "*Behave!* Or you'll go to the principal's office! Miss Pepper doesn't like it when people talk out!"

Hannah's grandmother wrote "dog."

"This test is very easy, teacher," she said.

"Call me *Miss Pepper*!" said Hannah. "You talked out again! And you didn't raise your hand!" Hannah got a funny expression on her face. "And this test is *not* so easy," she said.

She reached over and took out the little comb that held her grandmother's bun in place. She held it up.

"Ten," said Hannah to her grandmother. *"Comb!"*

Her grandmother looked surprised. Hannah tucked the comb back in quickly before the bun had time to fall down loose.

Her grandmother leaned forward and wrote again.

"All right, class," said Hannah. She clapped again. "Sit up tall and pass in your papers."

"Should I collect?" asked Hannah's grandmother.

BOWKNOTS
Kasha
SALT
Bread
SCHOOL

"No," said Hannah. "Not today, Trudy. You talked too much and you didn't raise your hand. You forgot Miss Pepper's rules of classroom behavior. So you can't get a gold star on your paper. And you can't be the monitor today."

"So who will be the collecting monitor?" asked her grandmother.

"*I* will be the collecting monitor," said Hannah. "I will be Miss Pepper *and* the monitor."

She collected her grandmother's paper.

"All right, Trudy," said Hannah. "Your paper is on top. So I'll correct it first. Let's see now:

"One: book, b-o-o-k. Correct."

"Two: hat, h-a-t. Correct."

"Three: hand, h-a-n-d. Correct."

"Four: me, m-e. Correct."

"Five: you, y-o-u. Correct."

"Six: girl, g-i-r-l. Correct."

"Seven: boy, b-o-y. Correct."

"Eight: cat, c-a-t. Correct."

"Nine: dog, d-o-g. Correct."

"Correct, correct, correct," said Hannah's grandmother. "Who can't spell those easy words? We did them many times."

"Just a minute, Trudy," said Hannah. "You're talking out without raising your hand again. And *we shall see*."

Hannah looked at her grandmother and frowned.

Her grandmother raised her hand.

"Yes, Trudy?" asked Hannah. "You have a question?"

"*What* shall we see?" asked Hannah's grandmother.

"Ten!" said Hannah. "Comb, c-o-m. Oh, Trudy, that's *wrong*!"

"Wrong?" asked Hannah's grandmother. "What is wrong?"

Now *she* took the comb out of her bun and held it up. She tucked it back in place quickly too before the bun could fall down. "Comb, c-o-m," she said. "How else?"

"C-o-m-*b*," said Hannah.

"C-o-m-*b*?" asked Hannah's grandmother. "C-o-m-b is combuh."

"But that's how you spell 'comb,' Trudy," said Hannah. "C-o-m-b."

"Impossible!" said Hannah's grandmother. "I know you're smart, Hannah, but I hope you don't think I'm a fool just because I wasn't born here. I'm surprised you would play such a joke on me. 'C-o-m-b' is combuh. Any dope knows that!" She got up out of her chair.

"Sorry, Trudy," said Hannah, "take your seat.

'Comb' is c-o-m-b and that's that. That's the American way!"

Hannah's grandmother walked out of the kitchen. The screen door slammed shut behind her.

"Hey!" yelled Hannah. She was so surprised she forgot to talk like a teacher. "You're not supposed to let that screen door slam shut. Hey, where are you going? The school bell didn't ring yet."

"I just quit school," called Hannah's grandmother over her shoulder. She was walking up the street.

Hannah sat down. She didn't know what to do. Her grandmother had always been such a polite pupil before. She almost never went out in the street. What happened?

"Oh well," thought Hannah. She tried to be calm like a teacher again. "Maybe she'll just take a little walk around the block and come right back. I'll correct her paper and have it ready when she gets back."

Hannah put a "C" for correct next to each of the first nine words and an "X" next to the last one.

She wrote "90%" at the top of the paper the way Miss Pepper did in school when you got one wrong.

Then Hannah felt sorry about giving a word she knew her grandmother wouldn't know. So she took a tiny box out of the big school box. The tiny box had a silver star on top. Hannah slid it open and took out one star. She licked it and pressed it down on the paper next to the 90%. She thought a minute. Then she took out another tiny box with a *gold* star on top. She took out a gold star, licked it, and pressed it down on top of the silver star.

When her grandmother still hadn't returned, Hannah wrote "Very Good" next to the gold star. Then she added "Anyhow."

She put the two tiny boxes away. She ran to the screen door and looked up and down the street. She didn't see her grandmother but she saw Otto. She didn't want Otto to see her. So she ran back inside. She took her grandmother's hat and put it back in the hall closet.

A minute later Hannah heard the screen door shut. This time it didn't slam.

She looked up and saw her grandmother walk into the room. Now her grandmother had a funny expression on her face.

"I walked up the street to ask your mother," said Hannah's grandmother, "and she said it's right: 'C-o-m-b' spells 'comb'! That's the funniest thing I ever heard, but you're right!"

"Well, after all, Trudy," said Hannah, "teachers are always right!"

Hannah's grandmother reached into the school box and took out a sheet of drawing paper. She rolled it up into a big ice-cream cone. She fastened it with a clip. Then she turned it upside down and put it on her head.

"What are you doing?" asked Hannah.

"Getting ready to sit in the dunce corner," answered her grandmother. "Don't you remember when your Miss Pepper told you they did this in the time of the Pilgrims? You told me about it on Thanksgiving. The same time when you told me about the Indians and the turkeys."

"Yes, but Grandma, I mean, Trudy, you only do it when the teacher makes you. I am not going to make you sit in the dunce corner. I gave you a word we didn't learn yet. It wasn't fair. Teachers should be fair."

"*Everybody* should be fair," said Hannah's grandmother. "But this time the pupil puts *herself* into the dunce corner."

She put a chair in the corner. She sat with her homemade dunce cap on her head.

"C-o-m-b," she said softly to herself, "is 'comb.' English is a very fancy language!"

Hannah looked at her grandmother. She looked funny and sad at the same time. Hannah rushed up to her with her paper.

"Look," said Hannah. "A gold star. 90%. 'Very Good Anyhow.' Don't sit in the dunce corner, Trudy. Let's draw pictures instead!"

Hannah hugged her grandmother. She felt sorry she had given her a hard word. She also felt sorry she hadn't let her grandmother be the collecting monitor before. She told her she could be the crayon monitor *and* the drawing paper monitor, too. "You can be both at the same time," she said.

Hannah's grandmother reached into the school box. She took out two big pieces of drawing paper and two big boxes of crayons. The crayon boxes said "48 Colors."

"You may pass them out," said Hannah.

"Okay, Miss Pepper," said Hannah's grandmother. "Let's make American pictures!"

They drew and drew. Hannah used all the colors in the box. After a while, Hannah's grandmother said, "Hannah, maybe you would like to ask your mother if you can sleep over after the carnival tonight. Maybe you would feel too tired to go home."

"Oh—*sleep over*!" said Hannah. "I'd love to!"

She jumped up. She tap-danced "East Side, West Side" and sang. "Look," she said to her grandmother, "shuffle off to Buffalo!"

"I'm really going to write a penny postcard to Hollywood and tell them my granddaughter takes tap-dancing lessons and she's better than Shirley Temple!" said Hannah's grandmother.

"Grandma!" said Hannah. "You always say that! Don't do it—I'm *not*!"

"But first I have to finish my gefilte fish," said Hannah's grandmother.

"Ugh!" said Hannah. She held her nose. "I'll be right back," she said. She started to run up the street.

Aggie Branagan's mother was outside sweeping the sidewalk.

"Hello, Mrs. Branagan!" said Hannah. "I'm going to the carnival with my grandmother! Is Aggie going?"

"Aggie has to clean her room today," said Mrs. Branagan. "Her room is a mess. If I've told that girl once, I've told her a hundred times: *Cleanliness is next to godliness!*"

"Good-bye, Mrs. Branagan!" said Hannah. She started to run again.

She ran until she came to the tree with the sign again. This time Otto wasn't in front of the sign. But his mother was. So was Frankie Cannelli's mother. They were yelling at each other.

"Your Otto is a rotten kid!" yelled Mrs. Cannelli.

"My Otto is a little gentleman!" Mrs. Zimmer yelled back.

"Mrs. Zimmer! Mrs. Cannelli! I'm going to the carnival with my grandmother!" said Hannah. But

they were so busy yelling, they didn't even hear her.

Hannah kept running up the street. She ran inside her house and said to her mother, "Grandma wants to know if I can sleep over after the carnival! Mrs. Branagan is sweeping the sidewalk again. I had to run so she wouldn't make another speech about keeping clean! And Mrs. Zimmer and Mrs. Cannelli are hollering at each other out in the street!"

"All right," said Hannah's mother, "you can sleep over. But keep calm. You're all out of breath again. You know what happens when you get overexcited or eat junk like hot dogs. Like what happened you-know-where."

"Please don't say 'you know what happened' and 'you-know-where.' It's embarrassing!"

"Okay, but just remember that hot dogs don't agree with you. So control yourself and don't beg for them. As for Mrs. Branagan, one of these days she'll take that broom and sweep out *Mr.* Branagan."

"*Why?* I *like* Mr. Branagan. He's nice. He's my favorite person on the street!"

"Mrs. Branagan has a hard life."

"Oh, no—not that again!"

"Okay, so not that again. As for the neighbors

hollering at each other, that's not news on our street. It will be news when they don't!"

"I still wish Grandma would come out and say hello to them sometimes."

"Grandma is not comfortable with our neighbors. So remember not to call them over to her at the carnival. Control yourself tonight. Be a mensch!"

"You always say that! What's a mensch?"

"It's Jewish for *person*."

"I *am* a person. Isn't everybody a person?"

"A person who knows how to behave right."

"Oh. Okay—I'll be one!"

"By the way, don't you think it was a little mean of you about 'comb'? You know Grandma didn't go to school in this country."

"It *was* mean," said Hannah. "I was sorry."

"Did you tell her you were sorry? And did you *do* something about it?"

"Yes, I did. And I gave her a 90% and a gold star on top of a silver star and a 'Very Good Anyhow' to make up for it."

"Good," said Hannah's mother. "*That*'s being a mensch."

"See you later," said Hannah.

"Keep calm!" said her mother.

Hannah ran out the door and began dancing down the street.

She danced until she came to the sign and then she stopped. Mrs. Cannelli and Mrs. Zimmer were gone. Mrs. Branagan was gone too.

Hannah did a cartwheel.

"I'm going to the carnival! I'm going to sleep over!" she said out loud. She held her arms out wide and tap-danced in circles down the street. Then she saw Otto Zimmer looking out the window. Hannah stopped dancing fast.

"I hope he didn't see me!" she said to herself. But, "Look at Hannah!" yelled Otto. "She thinks she's Shirley Temple!"

"Oh, I do not, Otto! You think you're such a big shot!"

"I am!"

"I'm going to the carnival tonight with my grandmother!"

"Oh yeah! Are you going to throw up behind a bush again?"

Hannah felt her face get hot. "Don't you say that, Otto Zimmer!" said Hannah. "I'm sorry I even answered you. Every time I just *talk* to you, I'm sorry!"

"Hannah threw up at the strawberry festival!"

yelled Otto. "Ha ha, Hannah!"

"Sticks and stones will break my bones, but names will never hurt me!" Hannah called back.

"But they do," she said quietly to herself.

"Raspberries!" yelled Otto.

Hannah ran down the street to her grandmother's. She opened the door to the kitchen and ran in.

"Grandma!" she said. "She said yes again! Oh, that Otto Zimmer gives me such a pain. He always takes the fun away!"

"Ignore him," said Hannah's grandmother. "I saw him in the street myself before. When his mother and father are not giving him a smack, he is smacking someone smaller than himself. Such people in this neighborhood! Such bigmouths! Whatever you do, don't call them over to me at the carnival."

"I wish you could meet Aggie Branagan's father," said Hannah. "Then you'd like our neighborhood better. Aggie's father *never* yells. And he can talk really fancy—like a *movie star*! I *like* him!"

"Fancy shmancy," said Hannah's grandmother. "I don't want to meet anybody—not even movie stars! Here, look what I made for you while you were gone."

"Oh, griblach!" said Hannah. "Grandma, *thank you*!"

Griblach were little crisp chicken cracklings. Hannah popped one into her mouth and crunched on it.

"I love things that go *crunch*!" she said.

"I know," said her grandmother. "That's why I made them. But don't eat *only* the griblach. Eat a little of everything."

Hannah's grandmother set down a big platter with lettuce, tomatoes, cucumbers, radishes, and scallions. Next to it, she put a big bowl of cottage cheese. And a basket of crisp buttered rolls with poppy seeds on top.

Hannah ate a little of everything. She popped a griblach into her mouth after each bite.

"Mmm," said Hannah. She swung her feet. She crunched her lunch.

"Mmm," she said again. "It's so *delicious* when your grandmother lives on your street!"

AFTERNOON: THE STORY

"Okay, teacher," said Hannah's grandmother after lunch. "*Now* it's time for the story."

She took an apple from the icebox, and a tiny knife, and a fruit plate.

"Come into my living room," she said.

They sat down next to each other on an old sofa with big pink roses and little white antimacassars.

Hannah's grandmother took her paring knife and began to peel the apple.

"Let me see," she said, "what story shall I tell today?"

"Any story," said Hannah, "as long as it starts 'Once upon a time.' "

Hannah watched as her grandmother's knife began a journey round and round the apple. The tiny blade flashed silver in the sunlight. A ribbon of red began to hang down. There was crisp-looking white underneath the red. Hannah loved the way her grandmother could keep the peel all in one long curling piece till she got to the end.

She put her head on her grandmother's shoulder as she watched. She held her breath. Then she heard something.

"Grandma," said Hannah, "guess what I hear in the curve of your neck? I can hear your heart beating!"

"My heart is beating in my *chest*," said Hannah's grandmother. "You are hearing my pulse."

"What's 'pulse'?" asked Hannah. "It *sounds* like your heart."

"Remember last week we went for a walk down by the river and you showed me a little cave where you make an echo? We called 'Echo! Echo!' and it came back. Remember?"

"Sure I remember. I always yell 'Echo! Echo!' there."

"Well, my pulse is like the echo of my heart.

Here—catch!" Hannah put out her hands and caught the long curly apple peel just as it fell off the apple. She wound it in and out around her fingers. "Look at all my rings!" she said. Then she unwound it and ate it.

Her grandmother took the core out and cut the apple in half. She cut the halves in half, making quarters. They each bit into a crisp quarter of an apple.

"It's so juicy!" said Hannah. "I can hardly wait for the story!"

"I thought of a good one when I was walking down the street before," said Hannah's grandmother.

"Is it about the olden days?" asked Hannah. "Does it start 'Once upon a time'?"

"Yes," said Hannah's grandmother.

"My favorite kind!"

"I know."

They ate the last two quarters of the apple.

Then Hannah's grandmother began her story.

"Once upon a time, in the olden days when I was a girl, I lived in a little shtetl on the banks of a river in Poland."

"I know 'shtetl' is Jewish," said Hannah, "but I forgot what it means."

"It means a little village."

"Oh—now I remember. Keep telling me."

"The name of my little shtetl was Mogelnitzer and it was *really* little—just a small group of tiny houses near the water.

"The nearest city was Warsaw and it was very large. *My* grandmother lived in Warsaw.

"Well, this story I'm going to tell you is about the first time I went from Mogelnitzer to stay overnight with my grandparents in Warsaw.

"When we went to see them, we had to ride in a horse and buggy for a long time."

"Was it longer than when you lived in the Bronx and I used to ride the bus to the George Washington Bridge and then Grandpa used to take me on the subway?" asked Hannah.

"It was about as far as that, but the horse couldn't run as fast as a bus or subway, so the trip took longer."

"But riding in a horse and buggy sounds like fun," said Hannah.

"It was," said Hannah's grandmother. She began to laugh.

"What's funny?" asked Hannah.

"I did such a terrible thing to my grandmother that night. I remembered it when I was walking down the street before, after our American spelling lesson. It's a wonder my grandmother ever invited me again."

"What did you do?" asked Hannah. "I can't imagine *you* doing anything terrible, Grandma, ever. Please—*tell me the story*!"

"Well, I was just about as big as you. I was so excited about going to my grandmother's, I couldn't wait. It was a big thing in those days to go on a trip. Like I said, we had to hire a horse and buggy, and the horse had to go over the cobblestones. My mother took me. We rode and rode. When we finally got there, she brought me in. She talked with my grandmother till she told her all the news. Then my grandmother told my mother all her news. And then my mother went home.

"But first she said to me, 'Are you *sure* you'll stay all night with Grandma and you won't cry for me?' "

"Why did she think you would do that?"

"Because I never slept over at my grandmother's house before and I was never away from my mother and father overnight. And it was a long way from home. So I told her, 'Go home, I'm not a baby,' and she kissed me good-bye and she went."

"And then what happened?"

"And then my grandmother played games with me till it was time to make supper. Then my grandfather came home and we all had supper together. After we ate and washed the dishes, we played some more. Then my grandmother told me a story and then we went to bed."

"And then what?"

"Then in the middle of the night I woke up and started to cry, 'I want my mother.' "

"What did you do that for, Grandma? You told your mother you wouldn't do that."

"Well, when I woke up, the first thing I remembered was my mother asking me if I was sure I wouldn't wake up and cry for her. So I did!"

"You must have looked funny crying, Grandma!"

"Don't you cry?"

"Sometimes, but I'm little."

"At that time *I* was little."

"I can't imagine you being little."

"Why not?"

"Because you're a grandma!"

"So will you be a grandma someday, too, just like once I was little like you. Did you think I was *born* a grandma?"

Hannah was quiet a minute. Then she said, "And then what happened?"

"So *my* grandma said, 'Don't cry, Trudy, I'll give you a lump of sugar.' "

"A lump of sugar? A *horse* eats a lump of sugar!"

"In my little shtetl in Poland, there was no candy in those days."

"No candy!"

"That's right. If you got a lump of sugar once in six months, it was a treat to remember for the *next* six months."

"I can't believe it!"

"It's true."

"Did you stop crying? Did you take the lump of sugar?"

"No. As special as it was, I still said, 'I don't want a lump of sugar; I want my mother.' I started to cry even louder. I woke up my grandfather."

"What did he say?"

"He said, 'Stop crying, I'll give you a kopeck.' "

"What's a kopeck?"

"A penny."

"A *penny*? He wanted you to stop crying for a *penny*?"

"Yes. That was even better than a lump of sugar. It was the olden days. A *kopeck*, if you got once a *year*, you'd remember it for *two*."

"So did you stop crying? Did you take the kopeck?"

"No. I just cried louder. I yelled, 'I WANT MY MOTHER. I WANT MY MOTHER. I WANT MY MOTHER.' "

"You behaved terribly!"

"That's right!"

"I can't believe it."

"Everybody behaves wrong sometimes."

"But not *you*, Grandma. You're a *mensch*!"

"Even me. Don't you think I'm human? But here's a hug for saying that!"

"So then what happened?"

"So then they had to wrap me in a blanket and put my hat on my head. My grandmother had to get dressed and put a big shawl over *her* head. In the middle of the night we got a horse and buggy and rode over the cobblestones back to my house."

"Wasn't it scary in the dark?"

"I couldn't see anything except a little white moon high in the sky behind us. Whenever I turned around, the moon was still there. I said to my grandmother, 'The moon is following us.' "

"What did she say?"

"She didn't answer me. The only sound I heard was *klop klop klop*."

"What's *klop klop klop*?"

"The horse's hooves on the cobblestones."

"Didn't you hear anything else?"

"Yes. After a while I heard my grandmother. She said I could never come and stay overnight at her house again. She said a lot of other things under her breath that I couldn't understand."

"I'll bet she was mad at you!"

"I'll say she was mad at me. When we got to my house, she made the driver wait. Then she got out and threw me over her shoulder. I was wrapped in the blanket like a sack of potatoes. My hat fell off my head and I cried, 'I want my hat!' She had to bend down to pick it up. Then she dropped my clothes that she was carrying in her other hand. By the time she got to the door, she gave such a big bang with her fist, she scared my mother. My mother came running to the door in her nightgown with her hair hanging down and no bathrobe."

"What did *she* say?"

"My mother didn't say anything."

"Why not?"

"My grandmother didn't give her a chance. She said, 'Here's your *brat.* Don't you ever bring her over to my house overnight again.' "

"She called you a brat? Your grandmother called you a brat?"

"That's right."

"Did she kiss you good-bye?"

"She didn't even kiss my mother good-bye. She didn't even *say* good-bye. She just got back into the buggy. The horse went *klop klop klop* again and she was gone."

"Your grandmother was mean!"

"Not really. She was also human. It was because she didn't know what to do. Sometimes when people are angry, they say things they're sorry for later."

"What did your mother do?"

"My mother started to cry, she was so insulted at what my grandmother said. She took me in and put me to bed. *She* kissed me good night and then she went to sleep."

"Did you?"

"No."

"Why not?"

"I started to think."

"What did you start to think *about*?"

"I started to think about the lump of sugar. And the kopeck."

"So what did you do?"

"I called my mother. I said, 'I want a lump of sugar.' And she said, 'A lump of sugar? What do you think this is, your birthday or something?' "

"And what did *you* say?"

"I said, 'But Grandma said she would give me a lump of sugar.' And my mother said, 'But I am not your grandma.' And then I started to cry."

"And then what?"

"And then my father came in."

"Did you tell *him* you wanted a lump of sugar?"

"No, I told *him* I wanted a kopeck."

"What did *he* say?"

"He said, 'KOPECK! What do you think I am, a millionaire? What's the big idea in the middle of the night—it's almost morning. Hey, what are you doing here anyway? I thought you were at Grandma's.' "

"So?"

"So I said, 'Grandpa said he would give me a kopeck. I WANT A KOPECK! I WANT TO GO BACK TO GRANDMA'S HOUSE!' "

"Wow! You *were* a brat! I can't believe it!"

"Everybody is a brat *sometimes*! Didn't I tell you?"

"Even a mensch?"

"Even a *mensch* can be human!"

"Did you get it?"

"*Did I get it!* You should see how I got it! One smack from each of them, both at the same time!"

"Ooh! Terrible! Did you cry more?"

"No. I was a brat but I wasn't a dope. I didn't take any more chances. I went to sleep. And that's the end!"

"What a story! It's the best story I ever heard. Tell it again!"

"Some other time. Not now. Now I have to finish my fish."

"Fish! Grandma! After such a good story, *fish*?"

"Like you like my stories, Grandpa likes my gefilte fish. When I finish, if we have time, we'll bake apple dumplings. If not, we'll do it tomorrow."

After stories and playing school, Hannah loved baking with her grandmother. "All right," said Hannah. "But you have to promise to tell me the story again tomorrow."

"I promise." Hannah's grandmother took the fruit plate, the tiny knife, and the apple core. She went into the kitchen.

Hannah stayed on the old sofa with the big pink roses and the little white antimacassars. She kept thinking about the story. She leaned her head back against an antimacassar and closed her eyes. Pictures of her grandmother and her grandmother's grandmother lined up and started a parade inside Hannah's head.

"Wait, wait," she silently told the people in the parade. "Go slower!" She wanted to make it last a long time. As the characters went by, Hannah told herself the whole story over again. When she came to the end, she opened her eyes and went into the kitchen. Her grandmother was just washing up.

Hannah threw her arms around her grandmother.

"I love your stories!" she said.

"And I love to tell them to you," said her grandmother. "Now I have to do more cooking so supper will be ready when Grandpa gets home. Also so you and I can get an early start to the carnival if we're still going."

"*If* we're still going!" said Hannah. "What a thing to say!"

"How about getting your toothbrush and pajamas and bathrobe and slippers?" said Hannah's grandmother. "Then you'll have everything you need here."

Hannah started to run up to her own house to get her things.

When she got to the tree with the sign, she saw Aggie Branagan. Aggie was running too.

"Aggie!" said Hannah. "I'm going to the carnival with my grandmother! I'm going to sleep over!"

"Help!" yelled Aggie. She ran behind the tree. Hannah looked around and saw Mrs. Branagan running toward them. Mrs. Branagan waved her broom.

"Aggie Branagan!" she yelled. "You get back in the house this minute! You call that filthy room *clean*? That room is a *pigpen*!"

"All right, all right!" yelled Aggie. She ran back in her house again. Mrs. Branagan ran after her.

Hannah ran into her own house. Her mother was just beginning to make supper too.

"Mrs. Branagan is chasing Aggie with a broom again," said Hannah.

"So what else is news?" said her mother.

"I came to get my things to sleep over at Grandma's."

"Now remember," said Hannah's mother, "if you see the neighbors, don't pester them to come over to you and Grandma. And don't nag Grandma for junk like hot dogs, because they don't agree with you. And don't get excited. Remember . . ."

"I know, I know!" said Hannah. "So many remembers! I promised Grandma already about nagging and pestering."

"Okay," said Hannah's mother. "As long as you behave yourself."

"Of course I'll behave myself," said Hannah. "Don't I always behave myself?"

Hannah's mother didn't answer. Instead she said, "And try to eat a little of Grandma's gefilte fish when she offers it to you. It will make Grandma happy and it won't kill you."

"*That* wouldn't agree with me," said Hannah. "You know I hate gefilte fish."

"You don't know what's good," said Hannah's mother.

"Yes I do," said Hannah, "and it isn't gefilte fish."

"Well, just remember to control yourself."

"I *will*!"

Hannah kissed her mother good-bye. She took

her toothbrush and put it in a little brown paper bag. She took her pajamas and bathrobe and slippers and put them in a big paper bag. And she started walking calmly down the street to her grandmother's house.

Then she passed the big leafy tree with the sign "CARNIVAL IN THE PARK TONIGHT." She put down her bags. She looked around to make sure no one was watching.

Then she did a somersault.

EVENING: CARNIVAL AND KOPECK

Hannah burst into her grandmother's kitchen. The screen door slammed shut.

"The carnival! The carnival!" yelled Hannah. "I can't wait!"

"Halloo," called a voice from the living room. "Who is slamming the screen door?"

"Grandpa!" said Hannah. "You're home!" She ran into the living room and put her brown paper bags on the old sofa with the big pink roses and the little white antimacassars. It was Hannah's favorite place to sleep.

"Halloo, Aynickle!" said Hannah's grandfather.

" 'Aynickle' is 'grandchild,' I know," said Hannah, "but why do you always say 'halloo'? You're supposed to say *'hello.'* "

"Halloo *and* hello," said Hannah's grandfather. He bent down and gave Hannah a kiss.

"Your mustache tickles!" said Hannah.

Her grandfather picked Hannah up and threw her into the air.

"Grandpa!" said Hannah. "Stop it! You know I don't like that!"

Hannah's grandfather laughed. He caught her and put her back down. "Why don't you like it?" he asked. "I always catch you, don't I?"

"Yes," said Hannah, "but I still don't like it. Everybody always does that to me. *Miss Pepper* even did it yesterday when I asked her for homework for the summer. And Otto *saw*! On the way home he said, 'Hannah sailed through the air like a basketball!' And then he made that raspberry noise. He thinks he's such a big shot!"

"Ooh," said Hannah's grandfather, "then I won't do it anymore. I wouldn't want to make you feel like a basketball. I'm sorry. What's for supper, Trudl?"

"Why do you call Grandma 'Trudl'?" asked Hannah. "Her name is Trudy."

"But I call her Trudl because it rhymes with

strudel," said Hannah's grandfather, "and that's what I brought home for dessert tonight."

"Oh, *good*," said Hannah. "I like strudel. It's my third best dessert." She took her grandfather's hand and they went into the kitchen.

"Everything smells so good around here," said Hannah's grandfather. "What are we having?"

"For you and me, good nourishing things," said Hannah's grandmother. "Gefilte fish, chicken soup with noodles, chicken, carrots . . ."

"Ugh!" said Hannah. She made a face. "I hate boiled chicken and boiled carrots. And the gefilte fish is sitting in that terrible-looking *fish jelly* again. Blah! It makes me gag!"

"For you, dear teacher," said Hannah's grandmother, "spaghetti with stinky cheese."

"Hooray!" said Hannah.

Hannah and her grandfather washed their hands. Then they sat down to eat.

"Mine is better," said Hannah.

"Ours is more nourishing," said Hannah's grandmother. "*We* are eating my good home-cooked food. *You* are eating from a box and a can."

"But Grandma," said Hannah, "it's so delicious!"

"All right," said Hannah's grandmother. "Be happy."

"Hey!" said Hannah to her grandfather,

suddenly remembering. "We're going to the carnival!"

"The carnival!" said her grandfather. "Who's got strength for carnivals after being in the city all day?"

"*We* haven't been in the city all day," said Hannah, nodding at her grandmother. "We have strength. Grandma and me. We're going right after supper!"

"Right after I wash the dishes," said Hannah's grandmother.

"Why do you have to wash the dishes?" asked Hannah. "I can't wait."

"Because the dishes don't want to wash themselves," answered Hannah's grandmother. Hannah helped clear the table so they could go faster. Then her grandfather put a little white box on the table.

"You open it," he said.

Hannah took the red-and-white string off the box.

"Strudel," she said. "My third best dessert."

"At least eat a piece of apple strudel and a glass of milk," said Hannah's grandmother. "Then you will have *some* nourishment, anyway."

"Charlotte russes are first," said Hannah. "With whipped cream and a cherry on the top."

"I'll bring you one tomorrow," said her grandfather.

"Apple dumplings are second. Strudel is third. Third is good, too," said Hannah. She ate her strudel. She drank her milk.

After they finished, Hannah's grandmother washed the dishes. Hannah and her grandfather dried them. Then Hannah's grandmother went into the bedroom to change her dress.

At last it was time to go. Hannah's grandfather was sitting in his favorite chair next to the radio. Hannah went over to kiss him good-bye.

"Shhh!" said Hannah's grandfather. "News!"

"Oh, Grandpa, you and my mother and father and 'News'! Every night you listen to news. *We're* going to the carnival!"

"Shhh!" said Hannah's grandfather.

"WE'RE GOING TO THE CARNIVAL!" yelled Hannah. She did a little tap dance for her grandfather. "Shuffle off to Buffalo!" she said. She kissed him good-bye.

"Oh, what a kid!" said Hannah's grandfather. He kissed her good-bye. He said, "Go already!"

Hannah went. She danced on out the front door. The screen door slammed shut.

"Hey!" she heard her grandfather yell.

Hannah started walking with her grandmother.

She ran a little downhill. Then she ran back up and caught her grandmother's hand. She walked with her grandmother a little more. Then she ran down farther and turned around. She jumped in the air and clicked her heels. She ran back up and took her grandmother's hand again.

"Grandma, hurry!" said Hannah.

"What's the hurry?" asked her grandmother. "The carnival is not running away."

"But I can't wait," said Hannah.

They got to the bottom of the hill Hannah's house was at the top of. Then they crossed a street and started down another hill that came to the park.

When they got to the top of the park, Hannah stopped. She caught her breath.

"Oh, Grandma!" she said. "*Look*—isn't it *beautiful?*"

Hannah didn't know where to look first: at the park, the carnival *in* the park, or the Hudson River at the bottom of the park.

Colored lights were strung through the trees.

All the way down the hill were little wooden stands. They were painted pink and purple and yellow and orange. Each one had a sign and a big picture. She saw ICE CREAM, ORANGE DRINK,

COTTON CANDY, ROOT BEER, FROZEN CUSTARD, PEANUTS, POPCORN, BEER, and FRANKFURTERS!

Hannah tried hard not to look at the painted frankfurter.

At the bottom of the hill were the rides. The Ferris wheel was the biggest. It had white light bulbs going all the way up around it. The light bulbs were reflected in the river. Next to the Ferris wheel was the merry-go-round. Hannah could hear the music.

"I love that music!" she said.

The moon was low in the sky. It looked like a big shining pumpkin. The whole river was beginning to sparkle around the reflections of the light bulbs and the moon. The longer Hannah stared, the farther the sparkle spread. Soon it went all the way across to the other side.

"Grandma!" said Hannah. She took her grandmother's hand. She tried to pull her down the walk. "Look at all the people—listen to the music! Hurry!"

"I don't like hurries," said Hannah's grandmother. "Listen, Hannah, I think you're getting overexcited."

"No, Grandma—I'm not getting excited. I'm

calm. Look—look how calm I am. I . . . oh, *look*, there's Aggie! *Hey, Aggie!* Did you come all by yourself?"

"My *father* took me!" Aggie called back. "He's getting me something to eat."

"Oh, her father's here!" said Hannah. "Grandma, wait till you meet Aggie's father!"

"No meetings, please," said Hannah's grandmother. "That was one of the promises. No getting excited. No asking for hot dogs. And no calling

neighbors. *Remember promises, Hannah!*"

"But Grandma, you didn't meet Mr. Branagan yet. He's the best neighbor of all. You'll change your mind about our street when you meet him—you'll see. He wears beautiful clothes and he talks nice and fancy. You'll love him. There he is! Oh, isn't Aggie lucky? He bought her a *hot dog*!"

Aggie opened her mouth wide to bite into it. Hannah heard music again.

Hannah pulled on her grandmother's hand and tried to run forward toward Aggie and Mr. Branagan.

"Hannah, no pulling! No running!" said her grandmother. "I tell you you're getting overexcited. And no, she isn't lucky. Who knows what kind of junk is in that hot dog?"

Aggie's father turned around. He was wearing a white suit, a bow tie, and a straw hat. He had a frosted mug in his hand. White foam was running over the top. He smiled when he saw Hannah.

"Ah, hello to my favorite young lady on the block," he said. "Mademoiselle Hannah!" He tipped his hat.

"And this gracious lady must be Hannah's grandmother," he said. "Good evening, Madame. Pleased to make your acquaintance." He took off his hat and bowed.

"See?" whispered Hannah. "Didn't I tell you he talks just like a movie star?"

"I don't trust him," Hannah's grandmother whispered back.

Mr. Branagan took a sip from his mug. Some foam stuck to his mustache. He licked the foam off with the point of his tongue. "Ah!" said Mr. Branagan. "Superlative! Ladies, may I offer you some refreshment? Hannah, would you like a hot dog like Aggie? And, Madame, would you care to join me in a beer?"

Hannah looked at Aggie's hot dog. Aggie was just taking a bite. Hannah could hear it *crunch.* She saw the juice run into the roll. The mustard made her mouth water.

"Oh, Grandma!" said Hannah. "It looks so good, I just have to have a hot dog. This one won't have any junk in it, I just know. I'll chew it a lot. I'll eat it slowly. I won't get sick—oh, please say yes! You could have a beer with Mr. Branagan. Look how nice the foam looks on top of his mug—like the whipped cream on a charlotte russe! Isn't it pretty? Can we? *Can we?* Hey—*where are we going?*"

Hannah was sailing through the air again. But this time, she was not sailing high like a basketball. She was more like a kite that left the ground but didn't rise. Her left arm was like the string. Her grandmother was pulling her *up* the hill! Hannah was gasping for air as she went up instead of down.

"Where are we going?" asked Hannah upside down. "You didn't even answer him! We didn't even get down to the bottom of the hill to the rides yet! I didn't even get anything to eat at all! WE DIDN'T EVEN GO!"

All of a sudden, even upside down, she recognized Otto Zimmer. He was walking down the hill with his mother.

"Hey, look at Hannah!" yelled Otto. "She's upside down!"

Hannah's dress fell over her eyes and she couldn't see anything. She kicked and struggled.

"I see Hannah's bloomers!" yelled Otto Zimmer.

Hannah screamed.

Then Otto screamed. His mother smacked him, hard.

"Act like a *gentleman*!" said his mother. "You rotten kid!"

"Good!" yelled Hannah. "Now you won't be such a big shot, Otto Zimmer!"

"GRANDPA!" cried Hannah as she was carried inside her grandparents' house. "We didn't even go! Grandma didn't take me!"

"Shhh!" said Hannah's grandfather. "News!"

"I don't like that news," said Hannah. "It stinks!"

"What is this commotion?" asked Hannah's grandfather. "Is that a nice way to talk?"

"No, it's not," said Hannah. "I don't want to talk a nice way. Mr. Branagan talked a nice way and Grandma didn't even answer him!"

Hannah was tired from yelling and struggling. All of a sudden she just flopped down on the old sofa with the big pink roses and the little white antimacassars.

Her grandmother undressed her and put her into her pajamas. Hannah didn't even say, "I can undress myself." She was too tired. She thought she would cry. But instead she fell asleep.

In the middle of the night, she woke up. Everything was dark and everything was quiet. Hannah was covered with one of her grandmother's summer quilts. Her grandparents were asleep in the other room. Something was bothering Hannah but she couldn't think what. All of a sudden she remembered.

She sat up.

"Grandma!" she yelled. Hannah's grandmother came hurrying into the room.

"What is it?" she whispered. "Don't yell; you'll wake up Grandpa. He has to get up early to go to the city tomorrow."

"You didn't take me to the carnival!"

"It's the middle of the night!"

"You broke your promise! I don't like you anymore! I want to go home!"

"You'll go home in the morning. It's the middle of the night now."

"No, I'm going home *now*," said Hannah. Then she had an idea.

"Give me a kopeck," she said. "Then I'll wait till the morning."

"Be quiet, kopeck," answered Hannah's grandmother. "There are no kopecks here. This is America. C-o-m-b, America."

"I want a kopeck," said Hannah. She said it loud.

"I'll give you a penny," said Hannah's grandmother.

She looked around for her purse. "Just don't wake up Grandpa. He has to work tomorrow. Your grandpa does not have a school vacation."

"I don't want a penny. I want a kopeck. I WANT A KOPECK. I WANT A KOPECK. I WANT . . ."

"This is the last time you'll sleep here!" said Hannah's grandmother. She pulled Hannah out through the screen door. The screen door slammed shut.

"Halloo?" called a voice softly through the bedroom door as they went down the stoop. "What's the commotion?"

"You woke up Grandpa!" said Hannah.

Her grandmother pulled her up the street to her own house. She was dangling in the dark again.

"Combuh, carnival, kopeck!" mumbled her grandmother. "Who needs grandchildren anyway?"

"You're *stuck-up*!" cried Hannah.

Hannah's mother came to the door after the first loud knock.

"Here's your pest!" said Hannah's grandmother. "Keep her! I don't want her overnight again!"

"She didn't take me to the carnival!" said Hannah to her mother. Her mother took her into the house and closed the door.

"What happened?" asked Hannah's mother. "Did you get a stomachache and throw up again?"

"No, I didn't get a stomachache and throw up again," answered Hannah. "I didn't get anything to throw up *from*. She didn't even take me!"

Hannah's mother put her in her bed. "Quiet!" she said. "You'll wake up Daddy. No talking till the morning."

"I WANT A KOPECK!" yelled Hannah.

She got a smack in the behind instead.

“We’ll talk in the morning,” said her mother.

When she was all alone, Hannah put her pillow over her face so no one would hear her.

“I waited all day to go to the carnival!” she said into her pillow. “And now I didn’t go!”

And she cried.

THE NEXT MORNING

"What happened?" asked Hannah's mother the next morning.

"I don't want to tell," said Hannah. "Grandma promised to take me and she didn't. That's all. And she was stuck-up to Mr. Branagan."

"I thought you promised not to pester Grandma about the neighbors."

"But he wanted to buy us things—free!"

"Eat your breakfast and go apologize for whatever you did wrong," said Hannah's mother. "*Try* to behave like a mensch. As for Mr. Branagan, don't worry. He never remembers anything in the morning."

"I'm not hungry," said Hannah. She ate half a pancake.

"I can't eat any more," she said.

"You can't eat pancakes?" asked her mother. "When you can't eat pancakes, something is wrong."

"She promised to take me and she didn't. Grandma broke her promise!"

"Go over and apologize. And get your clothes that you left there."

"But she didn't take me to the carnival."

"Anyway."

Hannah walked very slowly down the street. She dragged her feet. She had never had an argument with her grandmother before. She didn't know whether her grandma would still be her same grandma.

Hannah turned around. Instead of going down the street, she went up the street. She passed her own house and crossed the street and began to walk farther up to the mountain road. She walked all the way up to the top. When she got to the top, she pushed through the waist-high grass till she got to her secret place. Then she sat down and let her legs dangle over the edge.

She looked down at the roofs of the houses and the tops of the trees. She saw sailboats on the river. She watched the sun sparkle on the river all around and in between the boats. And she said to herself, "Grandma didn't take me to

the carnival! I'm mad at her."

Hannah sat and thought of all the things she could think of that she was angry with her grandmother for.

"I didn't get anything to eat at all. Not even things that *weren't* junk."

"I didn't get to go on the merry-go-round."

"I didn't get to go up on the Ferris wheel."

"I didn't even get down to the bottom of the park to *see* the Ferris wheel and the merry-go-round."

"She said, 'Who needs grandchildren!' "

"She didn't answer Mr. Branagan."

"She called me a pest!"

Hannah looked across the river to the other side. Then she remembered a day when her grandparents used to live in the Bronx: They came out for a visit. They brought Hannah a charlotte russe with whipped cream and a cherry on the top. Hannah took her grandmother up to see her special place. She took her charlotte russe up, too, and ate it at the top of the mountain. Then her grandmother said she couldn't come up again because she was too old to climb mountains. But she said it was something lovely and she would remember it for the rest of her life.

All of a sudden Hannah realized something.

"I miss her!" she said.

Hannah got up and ran down the side of the mountain. She crossed the street carefully and ran down her own street. She ran past her own house. She kept running till she got to her grandmother's house.

When she got there, the kitchen door was open. Hannah stood on the back stoop and peeked in through the screen door. Her grandmother was baking apple dumplings.

"She didn't even wait for me!" said Hannah to herself. Hannah loved to bake apple dumplings as much as she loved to eat apple dumplings. She loved the smell of cinnamon, sugar, and apples all mixed together. She loved the little pieces of walnuts that her grandmother stuck into the dough to make it crunchy. She could picture the glazed cinnamon and sugar bubbles at the top of each dumpling. She could smell it all through the screen door.

She inhaled loudly.

"Doesn't that smell good," said Hannah. Her voice sounded very small.

Either her grandmother didn't hear her or she made believe she didn't hear her. Hannah's grandmother paid no attention to Hannah standing outside the screen door on the back stoop.

"Want to play school?" asked Hannah. Her voice was so high, it didn't even sound like her.

Her grandmother turned around and looked her straight in the eye. But she still didn't say anything.

"We could spell *oral* today," said Hannah. "It would be easy. You wouldn't have to do any writing. *Grandma—don't be mad at me!*"

All of a sudden, Hannah's grandmother pulled the little comb out of her bun. Her hair fell down loose and she let it. She held up the comb.

"Ask me," she said.

"Spell 'comb,' " said Hannah. She said it through the screen door. She was afraid to go in without being invited.

Hannah's grandmother pinned her hair up. "C-O-M-B-*B*!" she said.

"What's the second 'b' for?" asked Hannah.

"Silly teacher! That's the one I left out from yesterday! Why are you standing out there like a dope? Don't you see I *need* you to help me bake apple dumplings? Besides, how can you tap-dance without your tap shoes that you left here? I polished them up with a little Vaseline."

"Oh, Grandma—you're still my same grandma!"

Hannah opened up the screen door and ran inside.

The screen door slammed shut.

Nobody said anything. They just hugged each other, hard.

"I went up the street to look for you," said Hannah's grandmother. "But your mother said she sent you down here already."

"I was worrying," said Hannah, "so I went up to my secret place on the mountain instead."

"Why were you worrying?" asked her grandmother.

"I made a commotion. I was afraid you'd be mad. I broke my promise."

"I *also* broke my promise."

"I didn't behave like a mensch."

"I *also* didn't."

"We got mad at each other! We never got mad at each other before."

"It could happen again. Now that I'm living in the country and not the city, we see each other more."

"Oh no, Grandma. I don't want us to get mad at each other again. When I woke up this morning, I was sorry we got mad. How could it happen again?"

"I was sorry already before I got back into bed. But listen, Hannah—we're *all* human! To humans, anything can happen: You make mistakes, you get

mad, you get sorry, you get glad—all kinds of feelings. Don't your mother and father ever have arguments?"

"Yes, but I don't like it when they do."

"But if people are together a lot, it happens. Grandpa and I have arguments also. *Sometimes*, Hannah, it happens. If it happens *all* the time, that's a different story. But when it happens sometimes, it's natural. It's not a calamity."

"Well, next time we get mad, let's not tell each other."

"No, Hannah. It's always better to say how you feel."

"But we insulted each other."

"True. Nobody needs insults. So next time we disagree, we'll leave out the insults. But when you get angry—and *everybody* gets angry, Hannah—if you tell how you feel, you can make it go away. If not, it stays inside you like a lump. Who needs lumps? Here, here's the only good kind of lump: a lump of dough that I saved for your apple dumplings. Here are the walnuts. And here are two apples. Make your own dumplings."

"There's just enough dough for one."

"So make one dumpling. Wait, I'll take the core out."

Hannah sprinkled a little flour on her grandmother's breadboard. She rolled the piece of dough into a ball. She stuck the little pieces of walnuts into the ball of dough. Then she took her grandmother's rolling pin and rolled the ball of dough out flat and thin. She sat the apple in the middle of the dough. She sprinkled sugar and cinnamon into the opening. Then she wrapped it up and pinched the dough together at the top. Her grandmother put it in the oven next to the other dumplings.

"Oh, what a smell!" said Hannah when her grandmother opened the oven door. "I can't wait to eat my apple dumpling!"

"It will be half an hour yet," said her grandmother. "Then they have to cool off. Meanwhile . . ." Her grandmother took out a little knife and a fruit plate and the other apple.

"Come into my living room," she said.

"Aren't we going to spell oral?" asked Hannah.

"Later," said her grandmother. "But first a story."

"First a story?" said Hannah. "Which story?"

"Don't you know?" asked her grandmother.

"*The* story, again? Now—*first*?"

"What else and when else? Didn't I promise? Who says things must always be done in the same order anyway? A story can be an education too!

And tonight we'll go to the carnival again."

"We'll go again? But we didn't go at all yet."

"That's why we'll go again. Always try again—especially if you didn't get there yet. I forgot to tell you, my grandmother tried again. I'll make the story a little longer today and tell you."

"She did? You will? HOORAY! But what if the carnival was only one night?"

"The carnival is all week."

"How do you know?"

"When I went up the street and couldn't find you, I went down the street to see if I could find you. I didn't find you but I found the carnival. They were cleaning up from last night. And they were getting ready for tonight. I bought two tickets for the Ferris wheel and two tickets for the merry-go-round."

"You did?"

"Would you like to sleep over?"

"Would you let me?"

"I slept over at my grandmother's again."

"Wait. I'll tell my mother! Just let me change to my tap shoes. Oh, they're so nice and shiny, they look brand-new!"

"Good—you'll be all ready when I write my penny postcard to Hollywood."

"Grandma!"

Hannah tap-danced out the door. She ran back

in. She hugged her grandmother again. Then she ran back out and danced up the street. She put her pajamas and bathrobe and slippers in a big paper bag again. She didn't have to take her toothbrush because her toothbrush was still at her grandmother's. She kissed her mother hello and goodbye.

"Did you apologize?" asked her mother.

"We both did," said Hannah. She waved as she danced out the door.

She tap-danced in big circles down the street. She didn't even look around first to see if Otto was looking. She didn't care if he was. She just danced on down the street back into her grandmother's house.

"I think I'll brush my teeth with my toothbrush," she said to her grandmother. "I had to brush with my finger this morning! I'll only take a minute."

She brushed her teeth with her toothbrush.

She went into the living room with her grandmother.

She leaned back on the old sofa with the big pink roses and the little white antimacassars. She smelled the delicious smell from the kitchen. She watched her grandmother's tiny knife begin its journey around the apple. The blade flashed silver in the sun. The peel began to hang down.

"Once upon a time . . ." began her grandmother.

"Oh, I just *love stories*!" said Hannah. She jumped up and did a little shimmy dance and sat back down. Then she thought of something.

"Grandma," said Hannah, "what will we do if we see Mr. Branagan again? You said we should say our feelings: I felt terrible about Mr. Branagan. He wanted to *give* us something. I *like* him so much."

"I understand how you feel, Hannah. But what if somebody wants to give me something and I don't want it? And give *you* something you're not allowed to have?"

Hannah thought a minute.

"Well, couldn't we have something *else* instead? We could still have fun."

Hannah's grandmother thought a minute.

"Don't worry, Hannah," she said. "I won't take away the fun. So I'll have a *root* beer. You could have an ice cream."

"Oh, Grandma! You're *not* stuck-up—you're nice!"

"And you're not a pest—you're a mensch! You bring fun to a grandma—and you teach her new things. *Thank you, teacher!*"

Hannah rested her head on her grandmother's shoulder. Her grandmother's knife went round and round the apple. The ribbon of red curled around in one long piece and hung on till the end. Hannah put out her hands and caught it. She wound it in and out around her fingers.

"Look at all my rings," she said. Then she unwound it and ate it and listened to the story.